ONE SMALL STEP FOR SPORK

**For Jen, Joanne, and Juliana,
three superior life forms—L.H.H.**

**To Ben, beloved human brother and
fellow pickle connoisseur—J.W.**

Text copyright © 2018 by Lori Haskins Houran
Illustrations copyright © 2018 by Jessica Warrick
Galaxy Scout Activities illustrations copyright © 2018 by Kane Press, Inc.
Galaxy Scout Activities illustrations by Nadia DiMattia

Library of Congress Cataloging-in-Publication Data
Names: Houran, Lori Haskins, author. | Warrick, Jessica, illustrator.
Title: One small step for Spork / by Lori Haskins Houran ; illustrated by
Jessica Warrick.
Description: New York : Kane Press, 2018. | Series: How to be an earthling ;
12 | Summary: "Alien Spork finally earns his Solo Explorer's badge, but he
needs the cooperation of all his earthling friends to return to his home
planet for the ceremony"—Provided by publisher.
Identifiers: LCCN 2017027415 (print) | LCCN 2017039870 (ebook) | ISBN
9781635920284 (ebook) | ISBN 9781635920277 (pbk) | ISBN 9781635920260
(reinforced library binding)
Subjects: | CYAC: Extraterrestrial beings—Fiction. |
Cooperativeness—Fiction. | Schools—Fiction. | Humorous stories.
Classification: LCC PZ7.H27645 (ebook) | LCC PZ7.H27645 One 2018 (print) |
DDC [Fic]—dc23
LC record available at https://lccn.loc.gov/2017027415

10 9 8 7 6 5 4 3 2 1

First published in the United States of America in 2018 by Kane Press, Inc.
Printed in China

Book Design: Edward Miller

How to Be an Earthling is a registered trademark of Kane Press, Inc.

Visit us online at **www.kanepress.com**

Like us on Facebook
facebook.com/kanepress

Follow us on Twitter
@KanePress

CONTENTS

1. Light Years Away 11

2. Ketchup and Yarn 20

3. Truzzle Juice 30

4. In a Pickle 38

5. A Matter of Time 47

   Galaxy Scout Activities 58

***Collect all 12 of
Spork's adventures!***

Spork Out of Orbit

Greetings, Sharkling!

Take Me to Your Weeder

Earth's Got Talent!

No Place Like Space

Alien in the Outfield

May the Votes Be with You

Money Doesn't Grow on Mars

Planet of the Eggs

Parks and Wrecks

Librarians of the Galaxy

One Small Step for Spork

ONE SMALL STEP FOR SPORK

by Lori Haskins Houran
illustrated by Jessica Warrick

KANE PRESS
New York

Spork

Trixie Lopez

Mrs. Buckle

Jack Donnelly

Grace Hanford

Piper Cho

Adam Novak

Newton Miller

Jo Jo

REPORT TO TROOP

BEEP. BEEP. BEEP.

Guys, are you serious? I finally earned a Solo Explorer badge? This is cosmic!

Hang on. Maybe I'm dreaming. Let me pinch myself—

OW!

It's really happening, isn't it?

My very first Galaxy Scout badge.

Woohoo!

Knognackle!

HOORAY!

1

LIGHT YEARS AWAY

"Congratulations, Spork," said Trixie. "That's awesome!"

"Thank you!" Spork grinned. "I don't want to boast, but it's a V.I.P. badge. Very Improved Performance! My troop leader says I'm doing way better on Earth than I did on planet Trablax. It helps that I haven't accidentally blown up your moon."

"Er—right," said Grace.

"There's going to be a ceremony just for me." Spork felt as if he were walking on air. And not just because of Earth's weak gravity. "I'll show you the badge when I get back."

"What do you mean?" Grace asked. "Where are you going?"

"To my planet, of course," Spork said. "The ceremony is on Cosmo. It's happening in three Earth days!"

"Oh," said Grace.

Trixie crossed her arms. Spork knew that look. "Don't worry. I'll come right back!"

"You'd better!" Trixie said.

Spork led the way into the classroom. "There's just one problem," he said. "My

landing here was . . . a little bumpy."

Trixie nodded. Spork knew she had
been looking out the window the day
he crashed on the school playground.

"I need to fix my ship before I can go
home," Spork went on.

"Don't you have any Gloop left?"
asked Trixie.

Spork sighed. He had plenty left. He
had brought a big batch from Cosmo.

Gloop could fix anything just like brand new. It was just . . . so tricky to use.

"Remember my first day on Earth?" he said. "My Gloop turned Jo Jo's wood shavings back into wood!"

Spork looked at the class hamster, asleep on a fresh pile of shavings.

Mrs. Buckle had taken the chunk of wood out of Jo Jo's cage and put it to work as a paperweight.

"Maybe you shouldn't try it," said Grace.

"Of course he should!" argued Trixie. "He has to get back to Cosmo! How else will he get his badge?"

Trixie patted Spork on the shoulder.

"Don't worry. We'll help you. And we'll be super careful. What could possibly go wrong?"

Gulp. Spork could think of at least forty-two answers to that question.

That afternoon, Trixie wore a smug smile on her face. "I told you," she said. "Easy peasy!"

Spork had to admit his ship looked great. They had squirted Gloop on every crack and dent. The outside of the ship was perfectly smooth. And the best part was, nothing bad had happened!

Except a tiny drip of Gloop had landed on Grace's shoe. Now her left sneaker was stiff and new, while the right one was still comfy and old. Grace said she didn't mind, but Spork noticed she was limping a little, like she was getting a blister.

"Come on!" urged Trixie. "Try it out!"

Spork hopped inside his ship.

Trixie started a countdown. "Three . . . two . . . one . . ."

Spork's finger hovered over the ignition button. Grace covered her ears.

"BLAST-OFF!" Trixie cried.

Click.

Click, click, click.

Spork kept pressing the button, but nothing happened. "I don't get it," he said. "The Gloop should have made my ship good as new!"

"Too bad," said Grace. "Well, we tried!"

"Hold on," said Trixie. She knelt down

to sniff a patch of yellow grass under the ship. "What's this stinky spot on the ground?"

Spork took a sniff. Oh, no! He recognized that smell. "There must have been a crack in my fuel tank! The Gloop fixed it, but only after all the fuel dripped out."

"No problem," said Trixie. "There's a gas station down the street."

GAS? Sometimes Spork forgot that Earth was so far behind other planets.

"That won't work," he said. "On Cosmo, our fuel is made from one hundred percent recycled materials."

He tried to think. "I could ask my troop to bring more, but they'd never get it here in time for the ceremony."

Besides, he didn't exactly want to tell his troop leader that he had run out of fuel. What if Commander Slurpp changed his mind about the badge?

Spork's antennae drooped. His first Solo Explorer badge had seemed so close.

Now? It felt light years away.

2

KETCHUP AND YARN

"Good morning, third graders," said
Mrs. Buckle the next day. "I have a
special challenge for you. A scavenger
hunt!"

"Cool!" said Adam.

Spork perked up. A scavenger hunt
did sound cosmic!

Mrs. Buckle held up a piece of paper.

"Your goal is to find the thirty items on this list around our school. You have thirty minutes to do it."

"Whoa," Piper said. "That seems quick."

"Too bad it's not in Cosmo time," said Spork. "A minute on Cosmo is like an hour on Earth! Or is it a whole day? The time difference is so confusing."

"How can one person find thirty things in thirty minutes?" Newton asked.

Mrs. Buckle raised an eyebrow.

"Who said it has to be one person? If you want, you can work together. I'll give you a few minutes to talk it over."

The kids huddled together. "There are sixteen of us in the class," Adam said. "Let's break into four groups of four. Each group can take a section of the list."

"Make that *fifteen* of you," said Jack. "I want to find all the items myself."

Then he did his best Batman imitation. *"I do my best work alone!"*

"Fine," said Adam. "So . . . five teams of three people. If each team finds six items, we'll have all thirty!"

Spork joined a team with Piper and Newton. Adam gave them part of the list.

"An eraser? A mug?" said Piper. "Easy! Those are right in our classroom."

"We can get a ketchup packet from the lunchroom," Spork said. He liked ketchup, though Earthlings had strange rules about it. Why was it okay to put it on French fries, but not on ice cream?

"Yes," said Newton. "But where are we going to find a purple pen, a piece of yarn, and a flashlight?"

Before they could talk any more, Mrs. Buckle held up a stopwatch. "Ready? Set? GO!"

Everyone dashed this way and that.

"Got the eraser!" cried Newton.

"Here's the mug!" Piper added.

Spork tried to squeeze through the door toward the lunchroom, but kids kept streaming in the other way with scavenger hunt items. It was like trying to pilot a ship through the Klotidium meteor belt!

"Hold on! We need a system!" called

Trixie. "Let people *out* first. *Then* people can come in!"

Adam and Grace stepped aside. "Good luck!" they called as Spork, Newton, and Piper slipped past.

At the lunchroom, Spork plucked a ketchup packet out of a bin.

"What's next?" he asked, bouncing on all four toes. It was way more fun thinking about ketchup than fuel!

"The purple pen," said Newton.

"Hey, Principal Hale writes in purple!" said Piper. Then she blushed. "She doesn't just write notes when kids get in trouble. She writes good notes, too!"

Sure enough, Principal Hale had a box of purple pens on her desk. She was happy to lend one.

The art room was right next door.
Newton stuck his head inside. "Mrs.
Petti," he asked, "do you have any
yarn?"

"Of course! I use it for art projects."
Mrs. Petti pulled out a ball of red yarn
and snipped off a piece for Newton.

"Eleven minutes to go," Spork

reported. "We just need the flashlight."

"I'll bet the custodian has one," said Piper.

But Mr. Albert had already given his flashlight to Jack!

"Eight minutes," Spork squeaked. Then it hit him. The nurse!

"Mr. Greg used a tiny flashlight to check my eyes once after I played, um, a few too many video games," said Spork.

"Yeah!" said Newton. "I've seen him use it to look at people's sore throats!"

The kids burst into Mr. Greg's office.

"My flashlight? Sure. Just remember to bring it back. Oh, and wash your hands! Sneeze into your elbows! Get lots of sleep!" Mr. Greg called after them.

"Two more Earth minutes!" cried Spork.

Spork, Newton, and Piper rushed back to the classroom. They tossed their items onto the pile.

"Twenty-seven, twenty-eight, twenty-nine, thirty," said Adam. "WE DID IT!"

3

TRUZZLE JUICE

"Just in time." Mrs. Buckle clicked her stopwatch. "Thirty minutes on the dot!"

"What about Jack?" Spork asked.

The classroom door banged open. Jack staggered in. His pockets bulged. He gripped a potted plant in one hand and Mr. Albert's flashlight in the other.

"I—got—fourteen," Jack panted.
Then he collapsed in his chair.

"Not bad!" said Mrs. Buckle. She
gave Jack a minute to catch his breath.
Meanwhile, she wrote a very long word
on the board.

"Today's scavenger hunt was about
cooperation," Mrs. Buckle explained.
"That means working together toward

the same goal. I wanted you to see how much you could get done as a group." She smiled at Jack. "I didn't expect anyone to try it on their own."

"Not even Batman could have pulled that off," Jack said. "It was impossible!"

Everyone laughed . . . except Spork. He remembered his own impossible task. It was even more impossible today than yesterday. Now he only had *two* days left to get to Cosmo! He slumped in his chair.

"Great point, Jack," Mrs. Buckle said. "One person—even a very capable one—can't match the power of cooperation. Not that it's always easy to work together. What were some of your challenges?"

Piper raised her hand. "We had to be

COOPERATION

organized. Otherwise we might all have gone looking for the same items. Adam did a good job making teams."

"And we had to be orderly," Grace added. "If it wasn't for Trixie, we might still be stuck in the doorway!"

Stuck, thought Spork. *That's me*. He pictured his spaceship, marooned on the ground.

He had worked so hard for his badge.
He had paid attention to everything the
Earthlings had taught him. Not just how
to use ketchup. How to be generous and
responsible and brave, too. Sure, he still
made mistakes. But he had improved
a lot. Now he'd finally earned a Solo
Explorer badge . . . and had no way to
get it.

Spork slid under his desk. *PLOP*.

"Spork, are you okay?"

Spork looked up from the floor. Mrs. Buckle was crouched beside him.

"Oh, sorry. It's just . . ." Spork couldn't say any more. He had a lump in his throat. Kind of like that time he swallowed a piece of gum. Why did Earthlings make food that you could chew, but not swallow?

Trixie jumped in. "Spork won a badge," she began. She told the class all about the ceremony, and the empty tank, and the fuel made from recycled stuff.

"What kind of recycled stuff?" asked Piper. "Maybe we have something like it here on Earth."

Spork shook his head. "No way. See, on Cosmo we eat these things called truzzles. They're long, bumpy vegetables packed in sour green juice—"

"Ew," said Jack. "That sounds gross."

"Cosmonians cut truzzles up and put them on other foods. Or we munch them whole. But we don't drink the juice. We dump it out. That's what my ship runs on. Truzzle juice."

"Wait a second. He's talking about *pickles*!" said Adam. "Spork, we totally have those on Earth!"

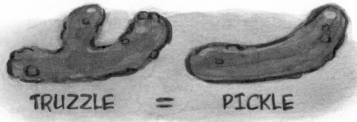

TRUZZLE = PICKLE

"And Earthlings dump out the juice, too," Piper added. "So people would be happy to give it to you!"

For a second, Spork perked up. *Could this really work? Could I make it to my badge ceremony?*

Then he shook his head again. "It would take a LOT of truzzle juice to get me back to Cosmo," he said. "One hundred Earth gallons! I could never collect that much truzzle juice in two days."

"You're right, Spork," Mrs. Buckle said, walking over to the chalkboard. "That's too much for one person—or alien—to do alone. If only there were another way." She tapped the word on the board.

"Cooperation! YES!" said Trixie. "All we need is a plan. Come on, guys. Let's get Spork some fuel!"

4

IN A PICKLE

"Spork, how does this look?" asked
Piper. She held up a bright green flyer.

GOT PICKLE JUICE?

DON'T TOSS IT! SPORK NEEDS IT TO GET HOME!

DROP OFF YOUR LEFTOVER PICKLE JUICE

AT THE SCHOOL PLAYGROUND

THIS SATURDAY, 10:00 A.M.

"Cosmic!" said Spork.

"We can hand them out around town after school," said Adam.

"I'll make copies in the office." Mrs. Buckle hurried out with the flyer.

"My story for the school newspaper is almost done," said Newton. "How's this for a headline? LOCAL ALIEN IN A PICKLE!"

"That's good!" said Trixie. "Can I use that on the morning announcements?"

"Sure!" said Newton.

Spork looked around the room. Everyone was so busy. Busy helping him! With the whole class cooperating, nothing felt impossible.

A hundred gallons of truzzle juice? Spork thought. *I could get a* zillion *gallons!*

Saturday morning, the playground buzzed with people, all holding jars of stinky green liquid!

Spork saw Principal Hale. And Nina from the comic book store. Even Mayor Tupper! Her jar had a fork in it.

"I ate the last two pickles on the way here so you could have the juice," she said. "We'll miss you. Hurry back!"

"I won't be gone long," said Spork. "I'm only staying on Cosmo for a couple of days."

"A couple of days?" said Grace. "But on your planet—"

"Here you go!" bellowed the fire chief. He passed Spork a huge jug of pickle juice. "We buy in bulk at the firehouse. Safe travels, Spork!"

"Thanks!" said Spork.

Spork toted the jug over to his ship. He climbed the silver steps and poured the pickle juice into his fuel tank.

SPLASH! The sound of the juice hitting the bottom of the tank was like music to Spork's ears. He could almost feel the badge on his uniform already!

SPLASH! SPLASH! SPLASH!

Spork could barely keep up with all the jars of juice coming his way. Jack, Newton, and Grace carried over one after another as quickly as they could. Grace seemed to run especially fast.

Oh, good. Her sneaker must not bother her anymore! thought Spork.

Trixie and Adam took the empty jars to the recycling bin. Meanwhile, Mrs. Buckle and Piper handed pickle-shaped thank-you notes to all the juice donors.

"How are we doing, Spork?" asked Trixie, stopping to catch her breath.

Spork peered into the tank. "Halfway there!" he said.

By eleven o'clock, the tank was three-quarters full. By noon, there were only ten gallons to go!

But why wasn't anyone passing him jars anymore? Spork looked around.

The playground was no longer buzzing. In fact, there were no more donors left. Not one!

Spork climbed down the steps. His friends gathered around.

"Did we make it?" asked Newton. "Did we get a hundred gallons?"

Spork shook his head.

"I don't understand," said Piper. "The whole town showed up!"

Grace seemed the most upset of all. Spork could tell she was about to cry.

He wanted to cry, too. His dreams of

his Solo Explorer badge were wafting away like a cloud of gas on Venus.

"I may not have a badge," Spork said. "But I have friends. True friends." He patted Grace on the shoulder. "Look, Grace has tears in her eyes. That's how much she wanted to help me."

Grace's face turned pink.

"Everybody tried their hardest," Spork went on. "Everybody cooperated. It just didn't work out."

He patted Grace again. Her face changed from bright pink to pale white. Then she burst out, "That's not true! Somebody didn't cooperate!"

Trixie turned to Jack with her hands on her hips.

"Hey, what are you looking at me

for?" said Jack. "I cooperated! I gave flyers to every restaurant in town. I even got Betsy's Diner to put pickles in everything to use them up!"

"He did," said Newton. "I had a bowl of pickle soup there yesterday."

Grace stomped her foot. "IT WASN'T JACK!" she shouted.

Spork stared at Grace. In all his time on Earth, he had never heard her yell.

Then Grace's voice dropped to the softest of whispers. "It was me."

5

A MATTER OF TIME

"You?" said Spork. "But I saw you. You were running really fast with the pickle jars!"

"Running the wrong way," said Grace. She hung her head. "When no one was watching, I hid most of the jars in the trees behind the playground."

Spork felt a pang in his chest. Grace didn't want him to get his badge?

"But why?" asked Piper.

"I don't want Spork to leave!" Grace said with a sob. She turned to Spork. "You say you're only staying on Cosmo for a couple of days. But time is different on your planet. A day there could be a month here. Or longer! We might be fourth graders by the time you get back. Or college students. Or grandparents!"

Trixie gasped. "I hadn't thought about that!"

"Spork, don't go!" pleaded Newton.

The others started chiming in, too.

"I won't be gone long. I promise!" said Spork. "Galaxy Scout's honor!"

"How can you be sure?" Grace asked. "You're always saying how confusing it is to figure out the time difference."

"I don't have to. I can just check my ship's tockometer," Spork said.

"Your ship's *what*?" asked Jack.

Spork had forgotten—again!—that Earth was behind other planets. How were Earthlings supposed to understand space travel when they had only visited their own moon?

"Tockometer," Spork repeated. "It

keeps track of time zones, no matter what galaxy you're in. I'll show you."

The others crowded around Spork's ship. He flipped a tiny switch, and a dial lit up bright purple.

"Tockometer, if I go to Cosmo for two days, how much time will pass on Earth?" asked Spork.

There was a loud whirring sound. Then the ship's computer began to talk.

"TRAVEL TIME TO COSMO: .5 EARTH DAYS."

"Half a day? That's not bad," said Trixie.

"*TWO-DAY STAY ON COSMO: 306 EARTH DAYS.*"

"That's *terrible*!" Trixie cried.

"Hang on!" said Spork. The computer wasn't done.

"*RETURN TRIP: .5 EARTH DAYS,*

MINUS 296 EARTH DAYS FOR PASSING THROUGH ZANDAR SPACE WRINKLE,

FOR A TOTAL OF. . ."

There was another whirring sound.

"*11 EARTH DAYS.*"

"Phew!" said Newton.

"Fascinating," said Mrs. Buckle.

"I'm sorry about what I did," Grace said. "I'm glad you're coming back soon!"

Grace hugged Spork tight. Everybody

else leaned in for hugs, too. Spork's heart was full.

But something else wasn't.

"Can we get the rest of the truzzle juice now?" Spork asked.

"Oh, yeah! Come on!" said Grace. She led the way into the trees, where pickle jars were heaped on the ground.

Everybody grabbed a jar and rushed back to Spork's ship.

"This should do it!" Spork poured in

the last jar. "YES—it's full!"

"Yahoo!" whooped Jack.

"I'd better get going if I'm going to make it to my ceremony on time," Spork said.

He was surprised to hear his voice shaking. He knew he wouldn't be gone long. Still, it was hard to say good-bye.

He looked at the Earthlings in front of him. Mrs. Buckle. Adam, Jack, and Newton. Trixie, Piper, and Grace. They

had been so kind to him ever since he crashed on their planet. They were some of his favorite beings in the whole universe.

"Wait! We have something for you!" said Piper. She held out a gift bag to Spork. Inside was the chunk of wood from Jo Jo's cage. Only, it was carved into a new shape.

"It's a statue of ME!" said Spork with a grin. Then he saw the words carved on the bottom. *For Spork, Honorary Earthling.*

Spork felt warm and happy all over, from his orange toes to the tips of his antennae.

"No matter where you go, you always have a home here, too," Newton said.

"So come home soon!" said Grace.

"Good luck! Good-bye!" the others called.

Spork climbed in his ship and closed the door. He waved to the friendly faces out the window.

Then he heard Trixie, counting down.

"Three . . . two . . . one!" she called. Spork pressed the ignition button.

BLAST-OFF!

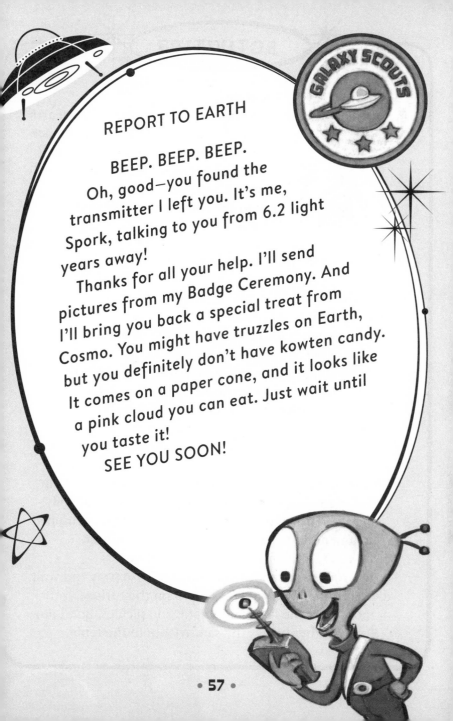

REPORT TO EARTH

BEEP. BEEP. BEEP.
Oh, good—you found the transmitter I left you. It's me, Spork, talking to you from 6.2 light years away!

Thanks for all your help. I'll send pictures from my Badge Ceremony. And I'll bring you back a special treat from Cosmo. You might have truzzles on Earth, but you definitely don't have kowten candy. It comes on a paper cone, and it looks like a pink cloud you can eat. Just wait until you taste it!

SEE YOU SOON!

ACTIVITIES

Greetings!
Without the cooperation of my Earth friends, I would never have made it back in time for my badge ceremony! Would you be able to earn a Galaxy Scout Cosmic Cooperator badge? Take this quiz to see how cooperative you are.
—Spork

(There can be more than one right answer.)

1. Your class wants to make a good-bye banner for a friend who is moving to France. You . . .
   a. Ask a teacher for paper and get the class to help you write "Bon Voyage!" ("Have a good trip" in French.)
   b. Hang up letters that spell "We will miss you!" Get each classmate to choose a letter to decorate.
   c. Make a banner by yourself. You'll get all the credit!
   d. Have each kid make a different banner to hang.

2. Your mom says you have to wait for lunch until she finishes making all the sandwiches. How can you help?
   a. Get ingredients from the fridge. Take out milk, jelly, turkey, lettuce, tomatoes, leftover spaghetti, whipped cream, and fish and put them on the counter.
   b. Go outside to play until lunch is ready.
   c. Tell your mom about your day while you sit and wait.
   d. Start an assembly line. You put on the turkey, your mom adds the lettuce, tomato, and pickles, and your little brother brings the sandwiches to the table.

3. Mrs. Buckle decides to host an awards ceremony. What can students do to cooperate in planning it?
   a. Work together to move the class furniture. One group moves desks and the other moves chairs.
   b. Make a list of snacks. Each kid can bring in one.
   c. Brainstorm a list of important people in the community and make invitations for them.
   d. Work hard in their most difficult subject to earn the Very Improved Person award!

4. After a storm, the playground looks as if a spaceship crashed into it! How can you cooperate to clean up?
   a. Invite friends to come and play on the playground.
   b. Write a letter to the principal asking for the mess to be cleaned up. Have your friends sign the letter.
   c. Organize a clean-up day. Get friends and families to help clean, rake, and plant new flowers.
   d. Ask to have indoor recess instead.

Answers:
1. Excluding people who want to help is not cooperative, so c is not the best choice. Choice d, making separate banners, is nice but not as cooperative as a and b.
2. Choice d, creating an assembly line, shows great cooperation. Pulling out the ingredients, as in choice a, can be a good way to cooperate, but make sure to find out what is needed (probably not spaghetti and whipped cream!). Choices b and c don't help your mom get the job done.
3. Both a and b are great because they show cooperation. If students make invitations, as in choice c, it is important that they work together on the list so they don't miss anyone and so no one gets more than one invitation. Working hard is always good, but d does not show cooperation.
4. A great way to get a big project done is by asking others to help, so c is good. A and d are not helpful, and b is not the best choice. Cleaning up would be more useful than working on a letter!

• 59 •

Spork's Sensory Scavenger Hunt

I set up a scavenger hunt for you! Work together with friends to find all of the items and you'll see how cooperation makes a task easier.

Can you find the items on my list in less than five minutes? GO!

Sight
- O Something shiny
- O Something transparent (see-through)

Hearing
- O Something that makes a soft sound
- O Something that makes a loud sound

Taste
- O Something that tastes sour
- O Something that tastes sweet

Touch
- O Something soft
- O Something rough

Smell
- O Something that smells like flowers
- O Something you don't like the smell of

Spork's Space Jokes

Q. What do you give a grumpy alien?
A. Some space.

Q. How do aliens get a baby to sleep?
A. They ROCKET!

MEET THE AUTHOR AND ILLUSTRATOR

LORI HASKINS HOURAN

has written more than twenty books for kids (not counting the ones her flarg ate). She lives in Massachusetts with five silly aliens who claim to be her family.

JESSICA WARRICK has illustrated lots of picture books about dogs, cats, and kids, but she is mostly interested in drawing aliens, for some strange reason. She does a pretty good job acting like an Earthling . . . most of the time.

Spork just landed on Earth, and look, he already has lots of fans!

★ **Moonbeam Children's Book Awards Gold Medal**
Best Book Series—Chapter Books

★ **Moonbeam Children's Book Awards Silver Medal**
Juvenile Fiction—Early Reader/Chapter Books
for book #1 *Spork Out of Orbit*

"Young readers are going to love this series! Spork is a funny and unexpected main character. Kids will love his antics and sweet disposition. Teachers and parents will appreciate the subtle messages embedded in the stories. The kids in the stories genuinely like each other, which I found refreshing. I will be giving these books to my young friends."—**Ron Roy**, author of A to Z Mysteries, Calendar Mysteries, and Capital Mysteries

"A breezy, humorous lesson in honesty that never stoops to didacticism. The other three volumes publishing simultaneously address similarly weighty lessons—lying, shyness, bullying, and responsibility—all with a multicultural cast of Everykids. . . . A good choice for those new to chapters."
—**Kirkus** for book #1 *Spork Out of Orbit*

"This is a book where readers, kids, and aliens learn together, experiencing how words and choices affect all of us. It's simple, elegant, and very insightful storytelling. *Greetings, Sharkling!* doesn't waste a single page of opportunity."
—**The San Francisco Book Review**

"I'm so glad Spork landed on Earth! His misadventures are playful and sweet, and I love the clever wordplay!"
—**Becca Zerkin**, former children's book reviewer for the *New York Times Book Review* and *School Library Journal*

"Kids will love reading about Spork. Parents, teachers, and librarians will love reading aloud this series to those same kids."—**Rob Reid**, author of *Silly Books to Read Aloud*

How to Be an Earthling
Winner of the Moonbeam Gold Medal
for Best Chapter Book Series!

Respect

Honesty

Responsibility

Courage

Kindness

Perseverance

Citizenship

Self-Control

Patience

Generosity

Acceptance

Cooperation

 To learn more about Spork, go to kanepress.com

Check out these other series from Kane Press

Animal Antics A to Z® (Grades PreK–2 • Ages 3–8)
Winner of two *Learning* Magazine Teachers' Choice Awards
"A great product for any class learning about letters!"
—*Teachers' Choice Award reviewer comment*

Holidays & Heroes (Grades 1–4 • Ages 6–10)
"Commemorates the influential figures behind important American
celebrations. This volume emphasizes the importance of lofty ambitions
and fortitude in the face of adversity…"—*Booklist* (for *Let's Celebrate Martin
Luther King Jr. Day*)

Let's Read Together® (Grades PreK–3 • Ages 4–8)
"Storylines are silly and inventive, and recall Dr. Seuss's *Cat in the Hat*
for the building of rhythm and rhyming words."—*School Library Journal*

Makers Make It Work™ (Grades K–3 • Ages 5–8)
Fun easy-to-read stories tied into the growing Makers Movement.

Math Matters® (Grades K–3 • Ages 5–8)
Winner of a *Learning* Magazine Teachers' Choice Award
"These cheerfully illustrated titles offer primary-grade
children practice in math as well as reading."—*Booklist*

The Milo & Jazz Mysteries® (Grades 2–5 • Ages 7–11)
"Gets it just right."—*Booklist*, starred review (for *The Case
of the Stinky Socks*); *Book Links*' Best New Books for
the Classroom

Mouse Math® (Grades PreK & up • Ages 4 & up)
"The Mouse Math series is a great way to integrate math and literacy into
your early childhood curriculum. My students thoroughly enjoyed these
books."—*Teaching Children Mathematics*

Science Solves It!® (Grades K–3 • Ages 5–8)
"The Science Solves It! series is a wonderful tool for
the elementary teacher who wants to integrate reading
and science."—*National Science Teachers Association*

Social Studies Connects® (Grades K–3 • Ages 5–8)
"This series is very strongly recommended…."—*Children's Bookwatch*
"Well done!"—*School Library Journal*